When Pigs Fly

by James Burks

Disney · Hyperion

Los Angeles   New York

First Edition, February 2018
10 9 8 7 6 5 4 3 2 1
FAC-029191-18012
Printed in Malaysia
Lettering and design by James Burks

Library of Congress Cataloging-in-Publication Data

Names: Burks, James (James R.) author, illustrator.
Title: When pigs fly / by James Burks.
Description: First hardcover edition. • Los Angeles ; New York :
    Disney-Hyperion, 2018. • Summary: "Henry is ready to do what no pig has
    done before. "But pigs can't fly," says his sister, Henrietta. Nothing
    will stop Henry from trying, until it looks as though gravity might
    finally get the better of him. Fortunately, Henrietta has an idea that
    gives both of them a lift"—Provided by publisher.
Identifiers: LCCN 2016033265 • ISBN 9781484725245
Subjects: • CYAC: Pigs—Fiction. • Flight—Fiction. • Brothers and
    Sisters—Fiction.
Classification: LCC PZ7.B92355 Wh 2018 • DDC [E]—dc23
LC record available at https://lccn.loc.gov/2016033265

Reinforced binding
Visit www.DisneyBooks.com

for Sienna and Axl

Today I will do what no pig has done before.

I'm going to FLY!!

But pigs can't fly.

It's easy!

You don't have wings.

Problem solved.

I have a bad feeling about this.

Maybe we should
fly a kite instead.

Once I'm airborne, just let go.

This jet pack

will do the trick!

Maybe I should wear the helmet.

Not flying.

Not flying.

UP!!

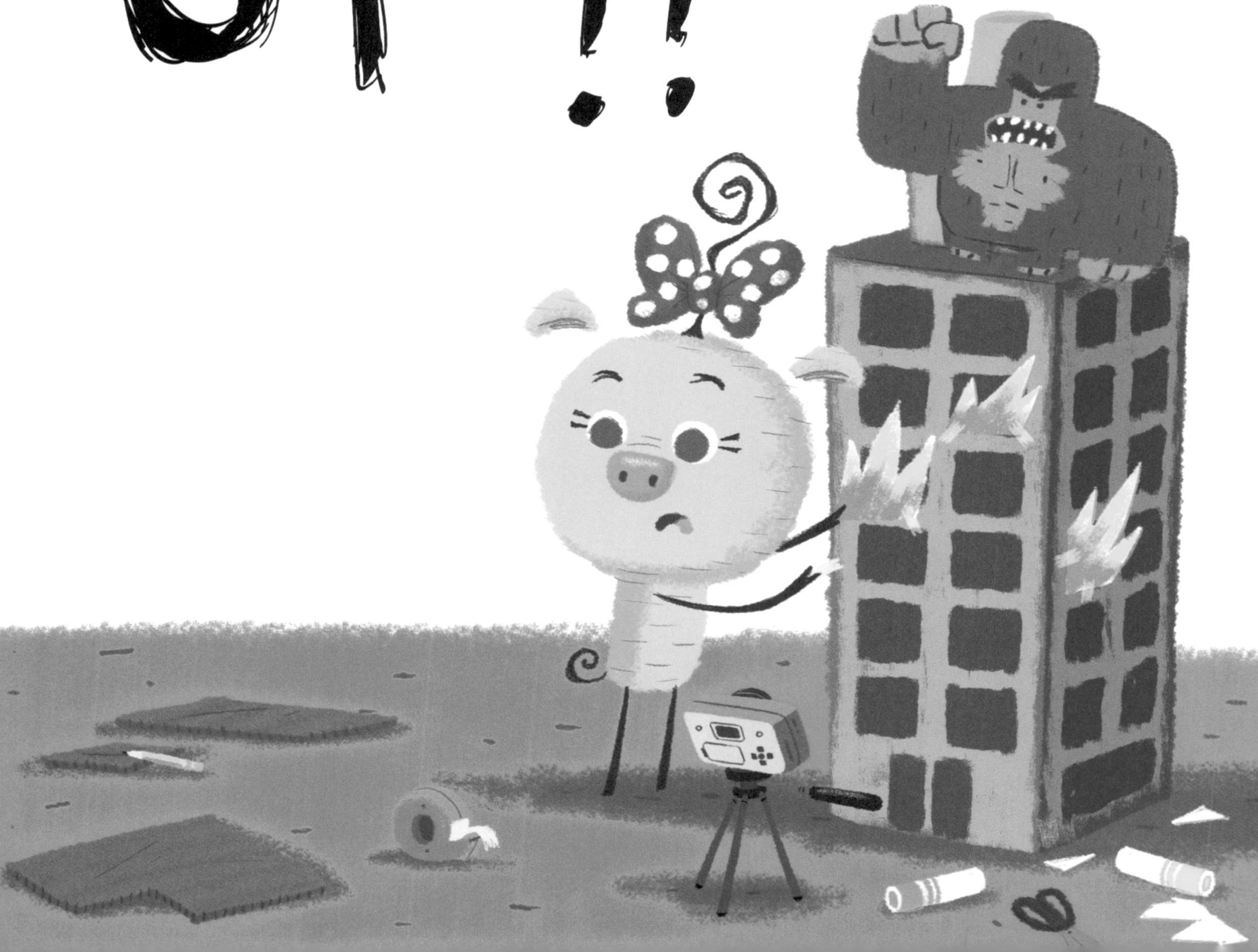

You're right.
Pigs can't fly.